Say hello to the new teacher

Dudley skidded to a stop outside Room 3.

Suppose my new teacher is old and ugly? Dudley thought. *Suppose she has hairy warts on her nose?*

R.J. joined him. "Why are you hanging around out here?" he asked Dudley.

"There might be a giant spider or a bug-eyed monster just waiting to eat us—"

R.J. wasn't listening. He was staring into the classroom, his jaw slack.

"What is it?" Dudley cried. He elbowed R.J. so he could stand in the doorway, too.

It wasn't a giant spider. Or a bug-eyed monster.

It was the new teacher.

She wasn't old and ugly. She didn't have hairy warts on her nose. In fact, she was the prettiest teacher Dudley had ever seen.

TEACHER'S PEST

TEACHER'S PEST

by Candice Ransom

illustrated by
Meredith Johnson

Troll

Text copyright © 1996 by Candice Ransom.

Art copyright © 1996 by Troll Communications L.L.C.

Published by Troll Communications L.L.C.

Printed in the United States of America.

10 9 8 7 6 5 4 3 2 1

Chapter

1

The Luckiest Boy Alive

Dudley Bobbin was building a tomb in his backyard.

"I have to hurry," he said to his dog, Barker. "This must be finished by nine o'clock."

It was the first day of school and Dudley didn't want to go. He knew he was getting the meanest teacher in the whole school, Mrs. Crump.

Mrs. Crump was about a thousand years old and never smiled, unless she had just failed someone on a test.

Dudley felt like the unluckiest boy in the world. He didn't like teachers as a general rule. No way was he going to put up with the meanest teacher in the school.

That was why he was building a tomb. He planned to hide out the entire school year.

Dudley got the idea of building a tomb from a movie about mummies. He used the huge cardboard carton that his family's new big-screen TV had come in. Turned on its side, the carton made a terrific tomb.

Tombs were supposed to be dusty, so Dudley emptied the vacuum-cleaner bag into the carton. Dust and lint flew everywhere. Barker sneezed.

With his markers, Dudley drew Egyptian symbols on the outside of the carton. He stood back to admire his work.

"Now all I need is a mummy costume," he told Barker.

Dudley went inside his house and pulled a bedsheet out of the dryer. The sheet had pink flowers on it.

"Oh, no!" he exclaimed. Whoever heard of a mummy wrapped in a pink-flowered sheet? But he didn't have time to find another.

Dudley ran back outside. He wound the sheet around and around himself, until only his eyes peeked out. Then he crawled inside his tomb and lay down on his back.

His feet stuck out one end. Barker sniffed his sneakers. Lifting his head, Dudley said, "Barker, go away!"

His dog wandered off in search of a squirrel to chase.

Dudley stretched out once more. He lay so still, he could hear his heartbeat. *Ka-thud, ka-thud.*

Even though his heart was beating, Dudley Bobbin was officially dead. He was a mummy buried in a dusty old tomb. No one would make a mummy go to school.

"Hey, Dudley!" a voice called.

Dudley knew that voice. It belonged to R.J. Turner. R.J. lived next door.

Dudley couldn't answer. Mummies did not talk. Barker came back and sat on Dudley's ankles. He forced himself not to twitch. Mummies did not move either.

He heard footsteps in the grass. Opening his eyes a sliver, Dudley saw R.J. bending down to look inside the tomb.

"Aren't you going to school, Dudley?" asked R.J. He wore his good school clothes. His backpack was hooked over his shoulders.

"Mmmmmddddd," Dudley said.

"What? Quit mumbling," R.J. said. "How come you're wrapped up in that sheet? Are you cold or something?"

Dudley sat up. It wasn't easy, since his arms were pinned to his sides. "MMMMMDDDDD!"

R.J. shook his head. "Can't understand a word you're saying."

Using his tongue, Dudley worked the sheet away from his mouth. "I said, I'M DEAD!"

"Why are you sitting in this box?" R.J. thumped the top of the carton. A shower of dust flew up.

Dudley coughed. "It's not a box," he explained. "It's my tomb. I'm a mummy. I've been dead a million years."

"You don't look very dead to me," said R.J.

"That's because you won't let me be dead! I was good and dead until you came along!" Dudley spluttered.

He and R.J. were the same age and in the same grade. But they weren't really friends. R.J. was too different.

Dudley liked to pretend he was an explorer. R.J. liked to read books.

Dudley liked to get dirty and run with Barker. R.J. always stayed clean.

Dudley liked to do things. R.J. liked to know things.

Like now.

"Why," repeated R.J., "are you sitting in a box?"

Dudley sighed. "Because I don't want to go to school, that's why. We're getting mean old Mrs. Crump." He knew that R.J. was going to be in his class this year.

"So?" R.J. asked.

"So I'm a mummy. Mummies don't have to go to school."

R.J. stared at the pink-flowered sheet. "I never saw a mummy in a flowered sheet before. They didn't have flowered sheets in Egyptian times."

"This is all I could find!" Dudley sighed. How could he be dead with R.J. bugging him?

R.J. glanced down the street. "It's almost time for the bus."

"I'm not going to school!"

"Not ever?"

"Not ever," Dudley replied firmly. "I'm staying in my tomb until the school year's over. Mrs. Crump will think I've moved."

"What about your parents?" R.J. pointed out. "Won't they miss you?"

Dudley hadn't thought about that. That was his problem. He often got neat ideas, but seldom planned very far ahead.

Of course his parents would miss him. They'd miss him at dinner.

"Tell them I ran away," he suggested. "If they don't look in the backyard, they won't know the difference."

R.J. snorted. "That's the dumbest idea I've ever heard. You couldn't stay in the backyard a whole day, much less a whole year."

Dudley squirmed. The sheet was hot and itchy. And he was thirsty. He doubted he would even last an hour.

"Well, it might have worked," he said.

Suddenly R.J. began to laugh.

"What's so funny?" Dudley demanded.

"I know something you don't know!" R.J. sang. "Something my mom found out."

"What?" Dudley asked. R.J.'s mom was in the P.T.A. Mrs. Turner knew all sorts of things about their school.

"Mrs. Crump isn't coming back this year," R.J. told him. "We're getting a new teacher!"

Dudley was overjoyed. "No Mrs. Crump! Whoopee! I don't have to be dead anymore!" He was no longer the unluckiest boy in the world. He was the luckiest boy alive!

Dudley did a little dance, even though he was hobbled by his mummy costume. His feet stirred up a smoky cloud of vacuum-cleaner dust.

He sneezed. Luckily, he was wearing a giant, pink-flowered handkerchief.

R.J. headed for the street. "Better not miss the bus!"

Dudley twirled like a top to unwind his sheet. He left it in his tomb, just in case he didn't like this new teacher either.

Then he ran through the back door, grabbed his backpack, and dashed out the front door. He still beat R.J. to the corner.

Serves him right, Dudley thought. *R.J. should have told me about the new teacher sooner.*

A real friend would have.

Chapter

Dudley the Dud

Dudley racewalked down the hall. Running was not allowed in school, but nobody said anything about walking very fast.

He skidded to a stop outside Room 3.

Suppose my new teacher is old and ugly? Dudley thought. *Suppose she has hairy warts on her nose? What if she makes me sit in the very front row?*

Dudley always sat in the back. He didn't want the teacher watching every little thing he did.

R.J. joined him. "Why are you hanging around out here?" he asked Dudley.

"You shouldn't rush into a new situation," Dudley said, quoting his favorite TV action hero. "There might be a giant spider or a bug-eyed monster just waiting to eat us—"

R.J. wasn't listening. He was staring into the classroom, his jaw slack.

"What is it?" Dudley cried. "Was I right? Is there a giant spider waiting to gobble us up?" He elbowed R.J. so he could stand in the doorway, too.

It wasn't a giant spider. Or a bug-eyed monster.

It was the new teacher.

"Wow," breathed Dudley.

She wasn't old and ugly. She didn't have hairy warts on her nose. In fact, she was the prettiest teacher Dudley had ever seen.

The teacher saw him gaping at her. "Do you belong in Room 3?" she asked.

"Yes," answered Dudley and R.J. at the same time. For a second, Dudley forgot R.J. was there, too.

The teacher smiled at them. "Please come in."

But Dudley was wedged in the doorway with R.J.

"I'll go first," offered R.J.

"No, *I'll* go first," Dudley said, pushing his shoulders through the door.

He spied an empty seat directly in front of the new teacher's desk. He sprinted toward it.

R.J. aimed for the empty desk, too. He reached the seat the same time Dudley did.

"This is my desk!" Dudley declared. He perched on the edge of the chair and stowed his backpack in the cubby.

"No, it's mine!" R.J. claimed the desktop.

"I'm sitting down," Dudley persisted. "See?"

But R.J. refused to unlock his death-grip. "Possession is nine-tenths of the law," he said.

"Well, I have the seat and that's worth—eleven-tenths of the law!" Dudley wasn't very good with fractions.

"Boys!" The new teacher came over. "I think the only way to settle this fairly is to let someone else have that seat. You each take different seats."

A girl with shiny black ponytails sat primly at the desk. "Do you mind?" she asked, handing Dudley his backpack.

Dudley glared at R.J. "The new teacher's mad at me and it's your fault!" He slapped his backpack on the desk behind Ponytails's desk.

"*My* fault!" R.J. plopped down in the seat across from Dudley. "You were the one yelling."

Before Dudley could argue further, the teacher closed the door. The first day of school was about to begin.

"Good morning, class," she said in a pleasant voice. "My name is Miss Swallow. I'm looking forward to spending this year with you."

Even though Ponytails's head was sometimes in the way, Dudley had a good view of Miss Swallow.

She was tall and slim and had long, red-gold hair. Her hair reminded Dudley of his golden retriever. Barker's fur was the same color.

"Let's get to know one another," Miss Swallow said, opening her attendance book. "When I point to you, please tell the class your name, and say something about yourself."

She pointed to the girl who sat in the first seat by the door.

The girl stared shyly at the floor and mumbled, "My name is Carolyn Beam. Um—I like to play with Barbie."

"Very good, Carolyn," Miss Swallow said. "Next? And

would you please speak up? I don't have your keen hearing," she added with a laugh.

This was a new way to call roll. Dudley learned all kinds of things about his classmates.

He learned that the ponytail girl who sat in front of him was named Kimi. Kimi had two guinea pigs and she watched her little sister sometimes.

He learned that Jake, the boy two seats over, wanted to be a comedian. He even learned that R.J. had a telescope.

Dudley looked at R.J. with interest. A telescope could come in handy on an exploration.

"Dudley Bobbin," called the teacher.

"THAT'S ME!" he bellowed. She wouldn't have to strain to hear him.

"You speak up just fine, Dudley. What would you like to share with us?"

Dudley thought. Should he tell Miss Swallow that he was an explorer? That his dog had the same color hair as hers? That he had built a tomb in his backyard that very morning?

There was no end to the fascinating facts about himself. It was hard to choose just one.

"I—" he began.

At that moment the bell rang. And rang.

The bell kept clanging.

Kimi clapped her hands over her ears. Jake opened his mouth like he was making the noise. Dudley thought that was funny.

Miss Swallow spoke over the racket. "Sit tight, class.

I don't think we're supposed to go anyplace."

"They're just testing the bell," R.J. told her.

Dudley frowned at him. R.J. thought he knew everything.

At last the ringing stopped.

"Where were we?" Miss Swallow asked. "Oh, yes. It was Dudley's turn."

But the bell still echoed shrilly inside Dudley's head. He couldn't remember what he had been going to say.

"We'll come back to you later, Dudley," Miss Swallow said, passing on to the next student.

He felt a jab of disappointment. That stupid bell had wrecked his moment!

After roll call, Miss Swallow remarked, "What an interesting class! I feel lucky to have such helpful, funny, and smart students."

Dudley knew the teacher thought that Kimi was helpful, and Jake was funny, and R.J. was smart. Miss Swallow didn't know anything about him, though.

She didn't know if Dudley Bobbin was smart or funny or helpful. Or all three.

He longed for another chance to impress her. He had never liked a teacher before. But he liked Miss Swallow.

Miss Swallow divided the class into study groups. Kimi, Carolyn, and Jake were in Dudley's group. R.J. was in another group. Dudley was glad.

"All right, class," said Miss Swallow, "let's move our desks together—"

Dudley didn't wait for her to finish. Here was his chance to prove to Miss Swallow that he was special.

He'd show her he was speedy and strong! That was twenty times better than being helpful or funny or smart.

Dudley leaped up immediately and shoved his desk against the back of Kimi's.

"Hey!" she said, annoyed by the jolt.

He pulled the desk behind into the back of his chair. He ran down the row, shoving each desk into the one before it. Soon his row looked like a train.

Quick as a deer, Dudley sprinted over to R.J.'s row and began pushing those chairs into a desk-train.

"Dudley," asked Miss Swallow. "What are you doing?"

"Moving the desks together, like you said." Now she would praise him for being fast and strong.

"Dudley, you didn't listen. I said to move your desks together *in groups*."

"Oh." He felt so dumb!

"Dudley the dud," said Jake.

Dudley didn't think that joke was so funny.

Helpful Kimi assisted the teacher. Smart R.J. showed them how to arrange each group of desks.

Dudley Bobbin just stood there, like a dud.

Chapter

3

The Fly-Tamer

"Oh boy, fingers-in-a-blanket! My favorite lunch!" Dudley pushed his tray down the serving line, bumping Kimi's tray on purpose.

"We're having *pigs*-in-a-blanket," she corrected him.

"Well, they look like fingers to me." Dudley took a plate heaped with little hot dogs wrapped in dough. "Look, that one still has the fingernail on it."

"Miss Swallow!" Kimi complained. Their teacher led the food line. "Dudley's being gross! Make him stop."

Dudley leaned forward eagerly. Would Miss Swallow scold him or just laugh? He didn't care, either way. But the teacher didn't do anything. She was busy chatting with the cafeteria lady.

With a sigh, he added a cup of Mexi-corn to his tray.

Dudley had a problem. He'd never had a problem like this in his entire life. He liked Miss Swallow. A lot. And he wanted her to like him back.

All that morning Dudley had tried to show Miss Swallow that he was different. But he could tell she didn't think about him one way or the other. He was just an ordinary kid in Room 3.

After turning in his lunch ticket, Dudley carried his tray to the table nearest the teachers' table.

Maybe he could choke or something and Miss Swallow would save him.

Kimi was already eating. She threw him a dark look. "If you're going to sit here, Dudley, you have to promise not to be gross."

"Okay." He began sorting through his cup of Mexi-corn. "I wouldn't touch the green things if I were you. The red ones are okay but the green ones—"

"Dudley, you promised!"

He grinned with a mouthful of corn, causing Kimi to scream. He hoped to cause a big ruckus at their table. Then Miss Swallow would notice him.

But the cafeteria was too noisy. He'd have to make a bigger ruckus.

R.J. came over, followed by Jake, Carolyn, and a girl named Marcy. They all sat with Dudley and Kimi.

Carolyn, Marcy, and Kimi began talking, ignoring the boys.

R.J. arranged the items on his tray in a circle, while Jake dug in as if he were starving.

"What are you doing?" Dudley asked R.J.

"My food is like a clock," R.J. explained. "The milk is at twelve o'clock, the silverware is at three o'clock, the corn is at six, and the pigs-in-a-blanket are at nine.

That way I can eat my lunch in order."

Dudley had never heard of anything so stupid. He reached over and dumped R.J.'s corn onto his pigs-in-a-blanket.

"What time is it now?" Dudley joked, expecting a big, disruptive laugh from everyone. A laugh so loud, Miss Swallow would have to rush over and quiet them down. Maybe she'd even take Dudley to the office.

R.J. glared at him. "Not funny, Dudley."

"Dudley does a lot of unfunny things," Kimi agreed.

"It's his talent," added Jake.

A talent! Dudley thought.

That's what he needed to make Miss Swallow pay attention to him. Being helpful was Kimi's talent. Jake's talent was making jokes. Even R.J. had a talent for always being right.

When the bell rang, Dudley dumped his trash quickly and raced back to the classroom. He had to figure out his talent and show it off to Miss Swallow.

"I'm passing out language arts workbooks," Miss Swallow said when the class was seated. "And then we'll move into our study groups."

Kimi waved her hand wildly. "May I help, Miss Swallow?"

"Of course. Who else would like to help?"

Before Dudley could raise his hand, the teacher chose Marcy. *Passing out workbooks is hardly a talent,* Dudley thought. *Anyone can do that.*

Real talent was something like . . . like being a lion-tamer. If only he could make a lion do tricks! But there was a shortage of wild animals in Room 3.

Dudley looked around, just in case he had missed one. Over his head, a fly walked on the ceiling.

A fly wasn't much of a wild animal, but it was better than nothing. What could he teach it?

Dudley rummaged in his backpack. He carried a small flashlight, like all explorers. Pulling the flashlight out, he switched it on and aimed the narrow beam upward.

The fly was in the spotlight. Dudley tried to get the fly to walk to the right. The fly followed the light! Then he made the fly walk to the left.

Maybe he could train the fly to perform a whole act. He could string a tiny little tightrope—

"Dudley!"

He jumped, swinging the light across the ceiling. The mixed-up fly flew in dizzy circles.

Miss Swallow stood by his desk. "Dudley, what are you doing? You're supposed to be in your study group."

"Look, Miss Swallow! I trained that fly up there. See, he walks when I move the light. I bet you didn't know I was so talented."

"I would say the fly is the talented one," she remarked wryly. "Now, put the flashlight away and join your group."

Dismayed, Dudley pushed his desk next to Jake's. "What are we doing?" he asked.

Kimi frowned. "You haven't heard a word the teacher said. We have to name our group. Does anybody have any ideas?"

"How about the Powernoids?" Jake said. The Powernoids were the hottest action heroes on TV.

"Yeah!" agreed Dudley. He traded high-fives with Jake.

"I don't like it," said Kimi. "And neither does Carolyn."

"Well, we like it," Dudley told her.

Carolyn spoke up. "We all have to like the name."

Dudley sighed. This could take forever. He needed to figure out a new talent to show Miss Swallow.

Across the room, R.J. raised his hand. "Miss Swallow, our group has a name."

"What is it, R.J.?" asked the teacher.

"T-Rex."

Miss Swallow wrote it on their study group chart. "Great choice," she commented.

Dudley was envious. R.J. would have to pick a cool name. It looked as if R.J. had a talent for picking names, besides being smart. No fair to have two talents!

"I gave my guinea pigs good names," bragged Kimi. "Want to hear? Salt and Pepper, because one's white and the other's black. We need to think of a good name like that."

Dudley was tired of Kimi's bossiness. Scrunching his nose, he snorted like a pig.

"Oink! Oink! Is that how your little pigs go?"

"They are *guinea* pigs, not real pigs," Kimi said.

He kept on making pig noises. "I think we ought to name our group the Hogs. What do you think, Jake?"

"Sounds okay to me." Jake was laughing at Dudley. "We even have a password!"

"Oink-oink-oink!"

Kimi was really mad. "Dudley, if you don't quit it—"

"Oink! Oink! Oink!" Now Jake was doing it, too.

Dudley bent over, pretending to root around for food.

"Does anybody have any old garbage for me to eat?"

Suddenly Miss Swallow was standing beside Dudley. "What seems to be the problem?"

"Him!" Kimi pointed at Dudley. "He's the problem, Miss Swallow!"

Dudley straightened up happily. At last he had the teacher's attention. Wouldn't she laugh when he told her their group was named the Hogs! And that they even had a password.

"Dudley Bobbin," Miss Swallow said sternly. "I know the first day of school is exciting, but you must settle down. Stop being such a pest."

Dudley was stung. The teacher called him a pest!

"Did you decide on a group name?" asked Miss Swallow.

Kimi shrugged. "The Hogs, I guess. Nobody can think of anything better."

Miss Swallow wrote the name on their chart. "At least I won't have trouble remembering it," she said, glancing at Dudley.

Dudley should have felt good that his name won. But he didn't have the heart to *oink* one more little *oink*.

"Miss Swallow liked our group name," R.J. commented as they moved their desks back. "She said it was a great choice. And I thought of it."

"She said she'd never forget ours," Dudley said, not to be outdone.

"Yeah, but yours wasn't great." R.J. looked very smug.

"Teacher's pet," Dudley jeered.

The fly buzzed around the room. Dudley wished he could train it to fly right up R.J.'s nose.

27

Chapter

4

The Gift

Dudley crouched low in the jungle grass. The Amazon River was full of man-eating crocodiles. If he swam really fast, he might make it across without being bitten in two.

Explorers faced danger all the time. It was their job. Explorers were tough, fearless—

"Hey, Dudley!" shouted a voice behind him.

Dudley jumped with a shriek. Then he was embarrassed. Explorers didn't shriek.

R.J. Turner broke through the bushes.

Dudley sighed. His game was ruined. Okay, the gully behind his house wasn't *really* in the South American jungle. And the trickle of creek water could hardly be the Amazon. But he'd been having fun. Leave it to R.J. to spoil Dudley's adventure.

"What are you doing here?" Dudley asked.

"Collecting leaves." R.J. picked up a broad yellow leaf. "I'm making a book."

"Did we have to do a science project?" Dudley didn't remember their teacher giving a science assignment.

The first week of school was over and so far Miss Swallow hadn't assigned much homework. Dudley was happy about that.

R.J. shook his head. "I'm doing it because I want to. I'm going to give it to Miss Swallow."

"You're giving the teacher a book of leaves?" Dudley had never heard of such a stupid present.

R.J. nodded.

Then Dudley was suspicious. Why was R.J. giving the teacher a present?

"How do you know she'll like it?" he asked.

"I don't." R.J. accidentally shredded the yellow leaf. "But I hope she will." He looked at the crumbled leaf. "Now I have to find another one."

"There's one over there, by that branch. You know," Dudley said thoughtfully, "we could hunt for leaves together."

Maybe they could *both* give the book to Miss Swallow.

R.J. was wary. "Well . . . okay. But it's still my book."

Dudley was good at finding different kinds of leaves. R.J. was good at knowing the names of different types of leaves.

"This is a poplar leaf. And this one is a sweetgum, I think. I'll have to check my tree book."

"Gee," said Dudley. "You know more about nature and stuff than anybody."

R.J. flushed. "I just read a lot."

When they had enough leaves, they went back to R.J.'s house.

"We'll work on the book together," Dudley said smoothly.

He cut squares of wax paper while R.J. made labels.

Mrs. Turner set up the ironing board and plugged in the iron. R.J. carefully pressed a leaf between two squares of wax paper. The heat from the iron sealed the leaf into a stiff page.

"Neat," Dudley commented. He would never have thought of making a leaf book.

R.J. stuck the labels on the correct pages, then punched holes along the left-hand side of each page. With yellow yarn, he began binding the loose pages into a book.

"Now let's make a cover for the book that says 'By Dudley Bobbin and R.J. Turner,'" Dudley said hopefully. "Then we'll give it to Miss Swallow together."

R.J. looked at him. "*I'm* giving it to Miss Swallow. Just me. It's my present."

"How come you're giving a present to the teacher anyway?" Dudley narrowed his eyes. "You have a crush on her, don't you?"

"I do not!" But R.J. spoke too fast.

Dudley knew he had hit on the truth. "I still think both our names should be on it."

"It's my book," insisted R.J.

"Well, I helped!"

"But I didn't ask you to," R.J. pointed out.

Dudley went to the door, indignant. "See if I ever help you again!"

Closing the door firmly, he stomped across the lawn to his own garage. Barker came over and sat beside him.

"That R.J. has some nerve, making a present for the teacher," Dudley complained to his dog. "He just wants Miss Swallow to like him best."

Barker tipped his head, as if asking a question.

Dudley never could lie to his dog. "Yeah, I'm jealous that R.J. thought of such a good idea. Maybe I should make Miss Swallow a present, too. Something better than a dumb old leaf book!"

Barker scratched his neck vigorously.

"Fleas bothering you again, boy? Okay, I'll comb you." Dudley liked to take good care of his dog.

From a shelf in the garage, Dudley took down a fine-toothed metal comb and a bottle of Spicy Lime after-shave. Then he squatted in the driveway and began combing Barker's red-gold fur. Barker pointed his nose blissfully toward the sky.

"Got one!" Dudley held up the comb. Caught between the metal teeth was a black dot. A flea.

Dudley pinched the insect between his thumb and forefinger. Because fleas were so flat, they were hard to squash. But Dudley had figured out another way to kill them.

He opened the bottle of aftershave. It was a brand his father didn't like, given to him one Christmas. Dudley knew he'd find a good use for it one day.

Now he dropped the flea into the pale green liquid. The black dot floated gently to the bottom.

"I bet I have a hundred in here now." Dudley recapped the bottle and shook it.

Black dots swirled like snowflakes. Slowly the dots settled on the bottom.

The best part was that the fleas were perfectly preserved in the aftershave. He could even see their tiny little legs waving in the fluid.

"Isn't it pretty?" he asked Barker, shaking the bottle again and watching with satisfaction. "It looks like one of Mom's snow globes, doesn't it? Only I guess you'd call it a flea globe."

Then he had a brilliant idea.

He would give Miss Swallow the flea globe! It was a much better present than R.J.'s leaf book. He bet his teacher didn't have one already.

"We need more fleas," he said. "Barker, sit still."

Dudley combed his dog over and over, picking out fleas and dropping them in the bottle.

In his house, Dudley found a box to put the bottle in and some leftover wrapping paper.

The paper had holly and Santas on it, but it was barely wrinkled. With a scrap of ribbon, he tied a clumsy bow.

Now, all he had to do was wait until tomorrow.

The next morning, Dudley met R.J. at the bus stop.

"Where's your leaf book?" Dudley asked him.

"Right here." R.J. patted his backpack.

Dudley shifted his own backpack carefully. Inside, the flea globe sloshed whenever he moved.

The bus pulled up. For once, Dudley let R.J. get on first. He wanted R.J. to pick a seat, so he could pick one closer to the door. He planned to beat R.J. to their classroom.

When the bus arrived at school, Dudley launched himself off the bus and down the hall to Room 3. R.J. was miles behind him.

"Whoa!" laughed Miss Swallow. "What's your hurry, Dudley?"

"I have something—" he gasped.

Just then an aide from the office interrupted to speak to the teacher.

Dudley fidgeted from one foot to the other. He was dying to give Miss Swallow her present.

R.J. came in as the aide left. He held out his leaf book to Miss Swallow.

"This is for you," he said, blushing. "I made it myself."

"With some help," Dudley put in, furious because R.J. had beat him after all.

"R.J., how nice!" Miss Swallow turned the pages of the leaf book. "It's beautiful. Thank you."

"Wait! I have a present for you, too." Dudley wrestled with the zipper on his backpack. He pulled out his gift and handed it to Miss Swallow. "Mine's *wrapped!*"

The teacher unwrapped the box. "And very well, too. Honestly, you boys didn't have to give me—" Opening the box, she lifted out the bottle of aftershave.

"Aftershave!" said R.J., laughing. "Boy, Dudley, don't you know what to give ladies!"

"It's not just that! Miss Swallow, shake the bottle." He was eager to see her eyes light up.

She shook the bottle. Black dots swirled in the pale green liquid.

"I'm afraid I still don't know what this is," she said, puzzled.

Dudley hopped with excitement. "Those are fleas! They came off my dog, Barker. You shake the bottle and watch the fleas go around—"

Crash!

The bottle hit the floor, smashing into pieces. Pale green liquid and dead fleas splattered far and wide.

The entire classroom smelled like Spicy Lime.

Chapter

5

Bellybutton Fuzz

"Ew, gross! There's a dead flea." Kimi pointed with the toe of her sneaker to a speck on the floor by her desk.

"It's just dirt. Mr. Gray cleaned up all the fleas." Actually, Dudley couldn't tell if the speck was dirt or a stray dead flea.

"He might have missed one," said Kimi. "And it still stinks in here."

The odor of Spicy Lime would be with them a long time. When the janitor had left with his mop and bucket, Dudley heard him mutter, "Never cleaned such a mess in my born days. Fleas and aftershave!"

Now R.J. leaned across the aisle. "You gave the teacher a terrible present. She couldn't get rid of it fast enough."

"That's not true!" Dudley retorted. "Miss Swallow didn't mean to drop it. She was just excited. She said she'd never seen anything like it."

"I guess not. It scared her." R.J. added, "She really liked my present."

Kimi twisted around. "What's with you two? Are you having some kind of contest over the teacher?"

"None of your business," Dudley said.

But he knew Kimi was right. He wanted Miss Swallow to like him best. But so far she seemed to like R.J. better.

"May I have your attention, class?" Miss Swallow went to the blackboard.

R.J. sat up arrow-straight, his hands clasped on his desk. He stared wide-eyed at the teacher, giving her his full attention.

Dudley sat up straighter. He sat up so straight he got a kink in his neck. He clasped his hands until his knuckles turned white and widened his eyes.

R.J. wasn't going be more attentive than he was!

"Parents' Night is next week," Miss Swallow said. "I thought it would be nice if you each wrote a poem to give to your parents."

Dudley twitched. He didn't like the sound of writing a poem.

Miss Swallow glanced at him. "Is something wrong, Dudley? You look very uncomfortable."

"No, Miss Swallow." It was hard to speak with his eyes bugged out like that. His eyeballs felt dry.

"Is there something in your eye?"

He shook his head, making his stiff neck snap.

Miss Swallow turned back to the class. "It really isn't hard to write a poem. I'll show you."

Picking up the chalk, she began writing on the board.

Dudley relaxed his eyelids in relief. He couldn't hold them open any longer.

"Who will read what I've written?" Miss Swallow asked.

R.J.'s arm flew up like a flag. He always raised his hand first.

Dudley flung his arm up, too. "Me! Me, Miss Swallow! Pick me!"

The teacher chose Carolyn.

In her small voice, Carolyn read, "'Crayons and paper, shoes and socks, pizza and cheese.'"

"What do those things have in common?" Miss Swallow asked the class.

R.J. knew the answer. "They all go together."

"Right!" praised the teacher.

Dudley frowned. One of these days, he would know the answer.

"This is how you will write your poems," Miss Swallow went on. "Write a list of things that go together. Let's have some suggestions to get you inspired. Marcy, can you think of two things that go together?"

"Kittens and whiskers?" said Marcy hesitantly.

"Good!" praised Miss Swallow. She pointed to Jake. "Jake?"

"Cars and tires!" Jake said.

Dudley was bored. He slouched in his chair the way he usually sat. Paying strict attention was tiring.

He lifted the hem of his T-shirt and examined his bellybutton. The little hole was packed with grayish fuzzy stuff. He picked at it with his finger.

crayons
paper
shoes
socks

pizza
cheese

What was it? he wondered. It looked like lint from the clothes dryer. Bellybutton fuzz, that's what it was.

Then he wondered if everyone had fuzz in their bellybuttons. Kimi probably did. And R.J., for sure.

"Dudley," said the teacher.

He hastily pulled his T-shirt down. "Yes?"

"It's your turn, Dudley. Name two things that go together."

"Bellybutton and fuzz," he blurted.

The whole class laughed.

Dudley felt his ears burn. He hadn't meant to say that! It just slipped out.

"Well!" said Miss Swallow. "You're certainly inspired, Dudley. Why don't you all work on your own? Write three pairs of things that go together. I'll be around to help."

Dudley pulled out a grubby sheet of paper. He didn't like writing poems.

Instead of working, he tapped his chin with his pencil. He tapped out "Jingle Bells." He could do all sorts of neat things. If only Miss Swallow knew!

R.J. hunched over his paper, printing furiously. He sat up suddenly and announced, "Finished!"

"So soon?" Miss Swallow asked. "Why don't you pass out these worksheets, R.J.?"

Dudley was jealous. R.J. always got to do stuff for the teacher. And he always finished his work first. No wonder R.J. was the teacher's pet.

While R.J. handed out worksheets, Dudley peeked at R.J.'s poem. R.J. had written:

Coming and going
Swings and kids
Backpacks and lunch boxes

What a dumb poem. Dudley could do a lot better.

Quickly he crossed out what R.J. had written. Then he printed:

Teacher and pet

R.J. returned to his desk. He stared at his paper. "Miss Swallow, somebody wrecked my poem!"

Dudley stared hard at his own blank paper.

R.J. poked his arm. "It was you, wasn't it, Dudley? You ruined my poem."

"I saw him," Kimi said. "Dudley scribbled on your paper, R.J."

"Traitor!" Dudley told her.

Miss Swallow came down the aisle. She glanced at R.J.'s poem. "Dudley, did you do this?"

He nodded reluctantly.

She sighed. "You've been very disruptive today, Dudley. I think you need to work at the quiet table."

Dudley despised the quiet table. There wasn't anybody to talk to or bug in the corner.

"Do I have to, Miss Swallow?" he pleaded. "I'll be good. I promise. I'll write my poem and—"

"Hurry up, Dudley," Miss Swallow said. "Take your paper and pencil with you."

He trudged to the back of the room and sat down at the lone table. There was nothing to do but work. Where was that inspiration Miss Swallow said he had?

He began writing all the gross pairs he could think of:

Slugs and slime
Sharks and teeth
Snakes and squeeze

"I'm done!" he cried. "Can I come back to my desk now?"

"Only if you apologize to R.J.," said Miss Swallow. "R.J., you and Dudley may sort this out, if you wish."

R.J. walked back to the quiet table. "Well?" he demanded. "Where's your apology?"

"Say I'm sorry to the teacher's pet?" Dudley exclaimed scornfully. "Never!"

"I'd rather be the teacher's pet than a pest!" R.J. hissed. Then he said loudly, "Miss Swallow, Dudley won't say he's sorry."

"Well, then, Dudley," said the teacher. "You'll have to sit at the quiet table the remainder of the day."

This is all R.J.'s fault, Dudley steamed. *A real friend wouldn't tattle.*

He added a line to his Together poem:
Friends and rats

Chapter 6

When Pigs Play Football

The next day Dudley saw R.J. waiting at the bus stop.

"Do you have to stand here?" He purposely stood as far away from R.J. as he could.

"It's a free corner," R.J. replied airily.

Dudley was still mad at him. Thanks to R.J.'s blabbermouth, he'd had to spend the whole afternoon at the quiet table. Why did the big rat have to live next door?

"I wish you'd move to another street," Dudley said.

"I wish you'd move to another state," countered R.J.

"I wish you'd move to another planet!"

"I wish you'd move to another solar system," R.J. topped neatly.

"I wish—" But Dudley was stumped. He didn't know what was higher than a solar system. He wasn't even sure what a solar system was.

R.J. grinned. "To what? Another galaxy? Another universe?"

"OH, BE QUIET!" Dudley cried, frustrated because his enemy had beat him again.

"You're just jealous because Miss Swallow liked my poem," R.J. bragged.

"She'll like my poem the best," Dudley said. "When I write it," he added.

R.J. snorted. "When pigs fly."

"What does *that* mean?" Dudley asked.

"Never, that's what it means," replied R.J.

Dudley glowered at him. R.J. always seemed so sure of himself. Well, Dudley would show him! By the end of the day, Miss Swallow would like Dudley Bobbin tons better than R.J. Turner.

At school, Miss Swallow announced a new project.

"Room 3 is going to put on a play for Parents' Night. We'll write our own script and make a set and simple costumes. Everyone will be in it."

Kimi raised her hand. "What kind of a play, Miss Swallow?"

"I think the class should decide," said Miss Swallow. "Let's have some suggestions and then you can all vote."

Dudley was interested. This sounded like fun. At least they wouldn't have to write any more poems.

"Who has an idea?" asked Miss Swallow.

Jake's hand waggled. "How about a soccer play?"

Miss Swallow wrote that suggestion on the board. "Anything else?"

Carolyn's hand went up. "How about a play about unicorns?" Carolyn had a unicorn doll that she sometimes brought to school.

"Unicorns," Miss Swallow repeated, adding it to the list. "Who else? R.J.? Do you have an idea?"

R.J. cleared his throat importantly. "I think we should do a play about what we're learning in class. How about a play on the presidents?"

What a boring idea! Dudley thought. *Only R.J. would drag schoolwork into something fun.*

"And who would you be?" he sneered. "George Washington?"

"I'd make a better George Washington than you would," R.J. retorted. "You don't even know where George Washington lived."

"I do, too. The White House!"

"Told you!" R.J. crowed. "It's Mount Vernon!"

"R.J. and Dudley," Miss Swallow interrupted. "No arguing. Dudley, do you have a suggestion for a play?"

"Umm—yeah."

Dudley knew he had to top R.J. or he'd be standing around on Parents' Night in a white wig and tight pants.

His gaze roamed around the classroom. On the wall hung the charts for each study group. Dudley's group was named the Hogs.

Hogs are cool, he thought. *Way cooler than presidents.* Too bad they couldn't do a play about pigs.

"Dudley, we're waiting," the teacher reminded him.

"How about—a pig play!"

Miss Swallow smiled. "A pig play?"

"Yeah." Dudley warmed to the idea. "We could do jokes and sing and dance. All pig stuff."

"Hey!" chimed in Jake. "I want to be a pig!"

45

"That shouldn't be hard," Kimi told him.

Jake made *oink-oink* noises at her.

"Settle down, class." Miss Swallow flicked the lights on and off. "Do we have any more suggestions?"

No one did.

"Then we'll vote on each idea. Let's see hands for the soccer play."

Jake started to put his hand up, then brought it down.

Miss Swallow wrote a zero by that idea. "The unicorn play?"

Carolyn, Kimi, Marcy, and three other girls raised their hands.

"How about the presidents play?"

"Booo!" Dudley said.

R.J. raised his hand solemnly, as if he were being sworn in.

"And last," said Miss Swallow, "the pig play."

All the other kids raised their hands. Dudley's idea won.

"Well, it looks like we're going to do a pig play." Miss Swallow dropped the chalk into the tray. "Let's think of some pig themes."

"'The Three Little Pigs'!" cried Kimi. "We could act it out."

"I want to be the big bad wolf," Jake said.

Kimi made a face at him. "I thought you wanted to be a pig."

Dudley was remembering a play he had been to with his parents. It was held in a restaurant with a stage. The actors served food between scenes. Dudley had liked that part.

"Miss Swallow! Miss Swallow!" he exclaimed. "How about if we have food? Like they do in plays sometimes?"

"Oh, you mean dinner theater. What do you think, class?" Miss Swallow asked.

Everyone agreed it would be fun to serve food.

Everyone but R.J. "We can't serve food," he stated. "It's against health laws."

"No, it isn't!" Dudley cried. "You don't like it because I said it!"

"Dudley and R.J.!" Miss Swallow looked annoyed. "I don't want to call you two down again. And it's perfectly all right to eat in our classroom."

"What are we going to eat?" asked Marcy.

Dudley had another idea. "I know! Garbage! We could make stew. Garbage stew!"

Miss Swallow laughed. "Dudley, that's terrific."

He wasn't done yet. "And we could call it Pig-Out Night instead of Parents' Night."

Miss Swallow was holding her side, she laughed so hard. "Pig-Out Night! I love it."

R.J. muttered under his breath. "Dumb, dumb, dumb."

Dudley didn't care about R.J. He was feeling great. Miss Swallow loved his ideas! He was sure she liked him best now.

They talked more about Pig-Out Night. First, they would sing "You Are My Sunshine," substituting "piggy" for "sunshine." Next the waiters would serve the garbage stew. The waiters would each recite a pig rhyme, such as "This Little Piggy Goes to Market." Then the actors would perform "The Three Little Pigs."

Miss Swallow began assigning parts. Marcy was chosen to be the announcer.

Jake was a good growler. "Rrrrrr!" he roared.

"Very good, Jake," Miss Swallow said. "You'll make a wonderful big bad wolf."

Kimi and Carolyn were Pig Number Two and Pig Number Three.

That left Pig Number One, the Head Pig. The Head Pig was the star. He outsmarted the big bad wolf. He also did the most singing and had the best lines.

Dudley was sure Miss Swallow would choose him for the part. After all, Pig-Out Night was his idea.

"R.J.," said the teacher. "Would you like to be the Head Pig?"

"Sure!" agreed R.J.

Dudley sat back, stunned. R.J., the Head Pig? It couldn't be true!

He raised his hand.

"Yes, Dudley?"

"Miss Swallow, are you sure you don't want to think it over?"

"You're not stealing my part!" R.J. whispered.

"The Head Pig is a very big part," Dudley went on.

"All the roles are important," Miss Swallow told him. "Remember, Pig-Out Night is a team effort."

Dudley slumped in his seat. He would get the starring part when pigs flew.

No, not even then. He wouldn't be the star if pigs won the Super Bowl.

Chapter

Hogging the Act

"Waiters," said Miss Swallow. "Positions, please."

Parents' Night was the next evening. The students of Room 3 were rehearsing their program.

"Hold up your arm," Miss Swallow instructed each waiter. "Just like you had a towel over it."

Five of the six waiters crooked their right arms, pretending to balance trays on their fingertips.

The sixth waiter put his hands on his hips and said, "Miss Swallow, are you sure you don't want me to be the Head Pig?"

Dudley still couldn't believe that he was a lowly garbage stew waiter.

"Dudley," replied the teacher wearily, "all the parts have been assigned. Now, waiters, make your entrance."

The waiters skipped in a line. Dudley hated skipping and dragged his feet.

The first waiter, a girl named Julianne, stepped forward and recited her rhyme. She ended by hopping on one foot and sweeping her hand behind her. The next waiter recited his rhyme, posed, and so on down the line.

Then it was Dudley's turn.

He clumped forward, gripping the slip of paper with his lines typed on it.

"'Pig's porridge hot, pig's porridge cold,'" Dudley recited woodenly. "'Pig's porridge in the pot, ninedaysold,'" he finished in a rush.

"Not so fast," Miss Swallow remarked. "It's not a race, Dudley. Do your ending. The others are getting wobbly."

But when Dudley hopped on one foot and held his hand out, he lost his balance and toppled over. His nose bumped the corner of the teacher's desk.

"Are you okay?" she asked, concerned.

"I think so." His nose felt flat. "Look, Miss Swallow! I'm the perfect Head Pig. I don't even need a mask."

"Quit trying to steal my part!" R.J. protested.

With her ruler, Miss Swallow waved at R.J. "R.J., let's hear your opening number."

R.J. stood tall. He had a real script, not just a slip of paper. "What page, Miss Swallow?" he asked.

Dudley blurted, "If I was Head Pig, I'd know what page!"

"Not another word, Dudley," the teacher said. "R.J., your song is on page two. Sing the first line."

R.J. drew in a deep breath, then let it out.

"Pigaro, pigaro, piii-gaaa-roooh," he sang in a rich, deep voice.

Dudley was surprised. He didn't know R.J. could sing like that.

"Let's try that once more," Miss Swallow said. "After the food is served, then R.J. starts his solo."

"When do we get to eat?" Dudley asked. He wasn't about to serve food and not have any himself.

"After the play has started, those waiters and actors not onstage can eat."

This play sounds more and more like hard work, Dudley thought.

"All right, R.J.," said the teacher.

"Pigaro, pigaro, piiigaarooh!" R.J. sang faster and faster. *"Pigaropigaropigaro."* Miss Swallow made up words to describe the stew. *"A bunch of bananas, an elephant's pajamas—"*

"Arrrgh, arrrgh, blaahhh!" Dudley sounded like a cat trying to cough up a hairball.

"Miss Swallow!" R.J. cried. "He's doing that on purpose!"

Whack! Whack!

Miss Swallow's ruler cracked the desk sharply. "Dudley, if you need a drink, please leave the room."

Dudley went out into the hall. He wasn't thirsty, but he didn't want Miss Swallow to know his coughing attack had been fake.

So far he hadn't convinced the teacher that he deserved to be Head Pig. What else could he do?

Next, the actors rehearsed the play "The Three Little Pigs."

Carolyn and Kimi, the other two pigs, sang with R.J.

Jake, the big bad wolf, growled like a greedy wolf.

Dudley watched his rival critically. R.J. could sing okay. But he wasn't a very good pig.

When the Three Pigs danced around, R.J. jerked along like a puppet. He wasn't the least bit piglike.

When rehearsal was over, Dudley shook his head at R.J.

"Nobody will think for a second you're a pig," he said.

"You just want my part!" R.J. accused.

"I can act better. Look, I'll show you."

Dudley pulled out his lunch box and opened the lid. He unwrapped his peanut butter and jelly sandwich. His mother had cut the sandwich in half, as always.

"It's not lunchtime," R.J. warned.

Smelling peanut butter, Kimi turned around. "I'm telling Miss Swallow."

Dudley opened the little plastic container of tapioca pudding and dumped it on top of his sandwich. He sprinkled cheese curls on top of everything.

"Ewww!" Kimi wrinkled her nose. "Are you really going to eat that mess?"

"You'll see."

Dudley clasped his hands behind his back. Then he pushed his face into the pile of food on his desk and began to eat.

"Gross," commented Carolyn, who was also watching.

"This is how pigs eat," Dudley said, his voice muffled.

"You really *are* a pig," R.J. said in disgust.

Miss Swallow marched down the aisle. "What's going on?"

Dudley lifted his head. Peanut butter and jelly were smeared on his chin. He had a cheese-curl mustache and tapioca in his eyebrows.

Miss Swallow stared at him. "Dudley!"

"I was just showing R.J. how to act more like a pig." He licked a glob of jelly from the corner of his mouth.

Miss Swallow crossed her arms, clearly upset. "You're certainly a good example. Dudley, since when are you the director of this program?"

"I'm not," he said sheepishly.

He wasn't the director. He wasn't the star. He was just Dudley, the pig's porridge waiter.

"Go wash up," Miss Swallow told him.

When he returned, the class was working on their Together poems.

"Copy your poems on this special pink paper," Miss Swallow was saying. "You'll each receive two sheets. Write your poems as neatly as you can."

Dudley's heart sank. He hadn't written a Together poem yet. At least, not a good one. He could hardly put that awful *Friends and rats* poem in his Parents' Night folder.

"Miss Swallow," he said, "I don't have a poem."

"Then that's your homework assignment tonight."

"But I'm not inspired." He was hoping she would let him draw a treasure map instead.

All Miss Swallow said was, "Kimi, would you please pass out the special paper?"

When Kimi gave Dudley his two sheets, she said, "I bet you mess up both of them."

Dudley stuck his tongue out at her. Those pig actors sure let fame go to their heads!

After school, Dudley went out to his tomb. He took his notebook and pencil.

"I have to write a poem," he said sadly to Barker. But he couldn't think of a thing to write. He was definitely not inspired.

Next door, R.J. came out onto his deck. He was carrying a long black tube on a three-legged stand. The telescope.

Dudley dropped his pencil. He wished he had a telescope. Every explorer needed one.

R.J. set up the telescope on one end of the deck. He twiddled with a knob, then peered through the lens.

Dudley couldn't stand it. Crawling out of his tomb, he crossed his yard into R.J.'s.

"Hey," he said. "What are you looking at?"

R.J. glanced up. "Oh, it's you," he said dully.

Without waiting for a invitation, Dudley hopped up on the deck. "Can I see? I won't touch anything."

R.J. moved aside. "Look through there."

Dudley squinted into the lens. The distant trees around the gully sprang into close-range view.

"Wow," he breathed. "This is really neat. But I thought people looked at the stars and planets."

"They do," said R.J. "Except—I don't really like to be outside at night."

"Boy, I do!" Dudley exclaimed. "I sleep out in my backyard all the time."

"I know. I see you." R.J. sounded envious. "You're always doing neat stuff."

Dudley wondered if R.J. wanted to explore with him. "Hey," he said. "I'm making up a new adventure—"

Just then the back door opened. Mrs. Turner stuck her head out and said, "R.J., time to practice the piano."

"I have to go," R.J. said to Dudley. "Have fun."

Dudley was glad he didn't have to practice the piano. He'd rather go exploring.

Then he had another thought.

Was R.J.—the star of the school play, the smartest kid in Room 3, and Miss Swallow's pet—jealous of *him*?

Chapter

8

Pre-senting Dudley Bobbin

When Dudley took his parents to Room 3, he didn't recognize his own classroom.

It was Parents' Night. The halls teemed with kids and grown-ups. Everything seemed different.

Small pots of garbage stew and pitchers of iced tea sat on Miss Swallow's desk. The scenery for the play blocked the blackboard. Real garbage cans held plastic bags of popcorn.

"My room doesn't usually look like this," Dudley explained to his parents.

The students' desks were set with red paper plates and flatware. On each desk was a pig-shaped folder.

"Where's your seat?" Dudley's mother asked.

"Right here." He showed them.

His father tapped the pig folder with Dudley's name on it. "What's this?"

"Nothing," Dudley said, flustered. "Just some dumb

thing we were supposed to write."

"I'd like to read it," said Mrs. Bobbin.

That won't take very long, Dudley thought. He wished he could hide the folder.

Just then Miss Swallow came up. "Dudley, it's time to get into your costume. Please make yourselves comfortable," she added to Dudley's parents.

Dudley hustled to the front of the room. Students were chattering and struggling into costumes.

"The Three Little Pigs" cast had real costumes. R.J. had buttoned his short felt coat wrong. He looked nervous.

"Waiters, over here!" called Miss Swallow. She handed them each a mask, a red bow tie, and a red cloth towel.

Dudley put on his mask. It was a pig face, made from a paper plate. He clipped on the bow tie and folded the towel over his right arm.

His parents were watching him. He was embarrassed to be a waiter in the school play. Especially a play that was his idea! But Dudley had bigger worries.

If his mother opened his folder, she wouldn't find a Together poem. She wouldn't find a poem at all.

His sheet of pink special paper was blank. And that was even more embarrassing.

"Okay, people," Miss Swallow said. "We're all set. Let's make this a great play!"

She switched on the tape player. Stately violin music poured into the room.

The guests settled down. Miss Swallow pointed to the announcer.

Marcy rang her bell. "Pre-senting Pig-Out Night in Room 3!" she proclaimed.

The entire class sang "You Are My Piggy."

Then Dudley and the other waiters made their entrance, carrying a poster with the menu lettered on it.

The grown-ups laughed when they read they were going to eat "pigatoni" pasta with tomato "slop."

When it was his turn, Dudley recited his pig's porridge rhyme. Then it was time to serve the food.

Dudley took one of the small pots of stew and a big spoon to his first table.

"Would you care for some stew?" he asked Carolyn's mother politely. *"Oink-oink,"* he added for good measure. After all, he was supposed to be a pig.

Carolyn's mother laughed. "I'd love some! Thank you."

Dudley spooned stew onto her plate, then went on to the next guest.

R.J., Kimi, Carolyn, and Jake were assembling at the front of the room. R.J. looked very important in his felt jacket with the "Head Pig" badge pinned on the collar.

If only I was Head Pig instead of a waiter! Dudley thought desperately. Then maybe his parents wouldn't mind so much that he hadn't written a Together poem.

"Would you care for some stew?" he asked Jake's father.

"Yes, thank you," the man replied.

At that moment, he noticed his mother open his pig folder. Without watching what he was doing, Dudley dipped the spoon into his pot.

"Young man!" Jake's father cried, jumping up. His

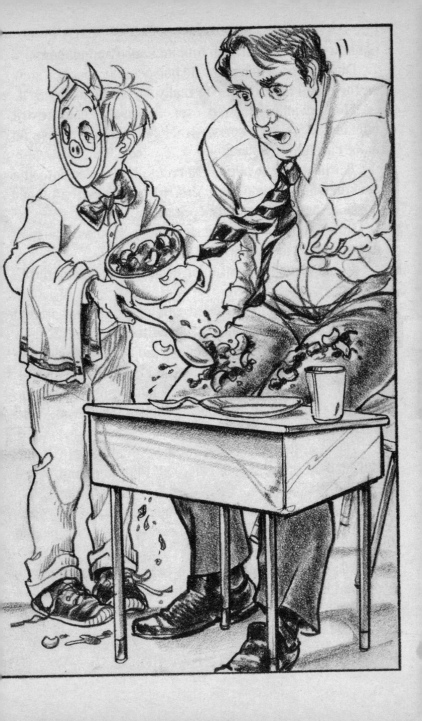

pants were plastered with tomato sauce and macaroni.

Dudley stared in horror. He had actually spooned stew on the man's lap! "Gosh, I'm really sorry," he apologized.

Miss Swallow hurried over. "Here are some extra napkins. We're very sorry, Mr. Hollis. Dudley, please be more careful!"

"I will, Miss Swallow." Nervous, he backed into the desk behind him, sloshing Mrs. Turner's iced tea on her purse. "Sorry!" he said to R.J.'s mother.

He couldn't do anything right! Miss Swallow was mad at him. She'd never like him best now.

"Don't forget to refill their drinks," she whispered to Dudley.

The other waiters were already carrying around pitchers of iced tea. Dudley rushed to get his.

When the guests had been served, Marcy jangled the bell. "Pre-senting 'The Three Little Pigs'!"

R.J. stepped forward. He smiled shakily as the parents applauded. Dudley realized R.J. was very nervous.

The star drew in a deep, swelling breath and let it out. But instead of R.J.'s rich voice, all that came out was a tiny squeak.

Miss Swallow nudged the announcer.

"*Pre*-senting 'The Three Little *Pigs*'!" Marcy repeated testily.

R.J. drew in another deep breath. This time when he opened his mouth, the only sound was a feeble croak.

Dudley nearly poured iced tea on his father's head. R.J. had stage fright!

How awful R.J. must feel! he thought. This was true embarrassment.

Dudley knew the solo backward and forward. Maybe he could help.

Holding his pitcher in front of his face, he began singing, *"Pigaro, pigaro, piii-gaaa-roooh!"*

People twisted in their seats, wondering where the voice was coming from. Dudley kept singing with his face hidden behind the pitcher.

R.J. gaped at him. Then, finding his own voice, he sang, too.

"A bunch of bananas, an elephant's pajamas—"

Dudley and R.J. performed the entire number as a duet. *Two voices sound even better than one,* Dudley thought.

"Pigaro, pigaro, peee-gaaa-roooh!" they finished, to enthusiastic applause.

The play was a great success. When the show was over, the parents stood to cheer the cast.

R.J., Carolyn, Kimi, and Jake linked hands and bowed.

Then R.J. said, "Dudley should be up here, too. The whole idea for Pig-Out Night was his."

"Go to the front, Dudley," said Miss Swallow, "and take your bow."

Dudley bowed with the rest of the actors. Then all the waiters and artists and singers and the announcer took a bow with Miss Swallow.

The parents got ready to leave.

Miss Swallow gave Dudley a big hug. "Thanks for saving the scene. It was great of you to help R.J."

"You're not mad about Mr. Hollis's pants?" Dudley asked. "And Mrs. Turner's purse?"

"Oh, Dudley." Miss Swallow laughed. "Some days I don't know what I'm going to do with you. But I don't know what I'd do without you, either!"

Suddenly Dudley felt very special.

R.J. came over. "Thanks, Dudley," he said. "If you want to borrow my telescope sometime, it's okay."

"Thanks. Now I can go on a real exploration!" Then he offered, "Why don't you come with me?"

"Okay!" R.J. looked happy.

Dudley felt terrific. He wasn't the smartest kid in class. Or the funniest. Or the most helpful.

He was Dudley Bobbin. And there wasn't anyone else like him in Room 3.

His mother and father were putting their coats on.

"Wait," Dudley said. He took the special pink paper from his pig folder and borrowed his father's pen.

Things that Go Together, he wrote.

   Pigs and garbage
   Teachers and students
   Dudley and R.J.

At last, he was inspired.